Dracula
STUDY GUIDE

Earle Rice, Jr.

GLOBE FEARON
EDUCATIONAL PUBLISHER
PARAMUS, NEW JERSEY

Paramount Publishing

The Pacemaker Classics Study Guides

The Adventures of Huckleberry Finn
The Adventures of Tom Sawyer
All Quiet on the Western Front
Anne Frank: The Diary of a Young Girl
The Call of the Wild
A Christmas Carol
The Count of Monte Cristo
Crime and Punishment
David Copperfield
The Deerslayer
Dracula
Dr. Jekyll and Mr. Hyde
Ethan Frome
Frankenstein
The Good Earth
The Grapes of Wrath
Great Expectations
Gulliver's Travels
Heart of Darkness
The Hound of the Baskervilles
The House of the Seven Gables
The Hunchback of Notre Dame
Jane Eyre
The Jungle
The Jungle Book
The Last of the Mohicans
The Mayor of Casterbridge
Moby Dick
The Moonstone
Narrative of the Life of Frederick Douglass, an American Slave
Oliver Twist
O Pioneers!
The Phantom of the Opera
The Prince and the Pauper
The Red Badge of Courage
Robinson Crusoe
The Scarlet Letter
The Sea-Wolf
A Tale of Two Cities
Tales of Edgar Allan Poe
The Three Musketeers
The Time Machine
Treasure Island
The Turn of the Screw
20,000 Leagues Under the Sea
Two Years Before the Mast
The War of the Worlds
Wuthering Heights

Supervising Editor: Stephen Feinstein
Project Editor: Karen Bernhaut
Editorial Assistant: Stacie Dozier
Art Director: Nancy Sharkey
Assistant Art Director: Armando Baéz
Production Manager: Penny Gibson
Production Editor: Nicole Cypher
Manufacturing Supervisor: Della Smith
Marketing Manager: Marge Curson
Electronic Page Production: A Good Thing Inc.
Cover Design: Dianne Platner
Cover Illustration: Karen Loccisano
Hand-marbled Paper: MOTH MARBLERS

Printed in the United States of America

2 3 4 5 6 7 8 9 10 99 98 97 96

ISBN 0-835-90959-X

GLOBE FEARON
EDUCATIONAL PUBLISHER
PARAMUS, NEW JERSEY

Paramount Publishing

Table of Contents

To the Teacher

The Content

The Pacemaker Classics Study Guides are a series of literature-based study units for secondary and adult students. Each study guide is designed to extend and enrich one of the Pacemaker Classics, though it may also be used with the original version of the novel. Each study guide includes teacher's notes and 35 reproducible student project sheets. Of these, 28 are based on units, or chapter groupings from the text, with 7 project sheets corresponding to each unit.

The pattern for these 7 project sheets is as follows: Unit 1: Setting the Scene, Prereading, Key Words, Point of View, Language Lab, Wild Card, and Challenge; Units 2-4: Prereading, Character Study, Key Words, Point of View, Language Lab, Wild Card, and Challenge. The Wild Card might be based on cause and effect, problems and solutions, analyzing plot, sequencing, extending the story, or any other skill that is suggested by the unit. The challenge activities are on a more difficult level than the other project sheets and are not necessarily recommended for all students.

A 2-page final exam follows the unit project sheets. The last 5 pages are open-ended project sheets, including activities for working with the glossary, sequencing the story, understanding the times, and writing a book report. These project sheets should be used after the students have completed the book.

Students should be provided with a copy of Teacher's Notes, page v (About the Author/About the Times). The information on this page is necessary for them to complete some of the open-ended project sheets.

The Methodology

A whole-language approach is implicit in the instructional design of this series. The reproducible exercise pages encourage students to use many forms of communication and draw on their prior knowledge to increase their enjoyment of the story, as well as their comprehension and thinking abilities. For example, a vocabulary-based project might include reading for context clues, as well as doing some creative writing using key vocabulary words. Thinking, reading, discussing, listening, and writing are only a few of the skills students will be practicing. This whole-language approach is designed to help students personalize and integrate what they are learning into their own lives.

This icon indicates any activities that are especially suited for cooperative group work. However, you may wish to organize cooperative learning groups or assign partners to work together for most or all of the activities.

Students will need to be familiar with terms like **character, plot, sequence, setting,** and **journal** as they do the worksheets. For this reason, a glossary of terms used in this book is included. You should duplicate this glossary and distribute a copy to each student.

Teacher's Notes

About the Author

Bram (Abraham) Stoker was born in Dublin, Ireland in 1847. He attended Dublin University before starting a career as a civil servant. In 1878, he gave up the civil service to become a business advisor and secretary to Sir Henry Irving—England's greatest Shakespearean performer and the first actor to become knighted.

Stoker worked for Sir Henry for the next 27 years, during which time he cultivated his talent as a writer. While employed by Sir Henry, he completed *Personal Reminiscences of Henry Irving* (1906), recollections of his life and duties with the noted actor. In *Reminiscences,* Stoker estimates that he wrote close to a half-million letters on Sir Henry's behalf.

Although handling the actor's affairs kept Stoker's work schedule quite full, he still managed to find time to write novels and short stories. In 1890, he wrote *The Snake's Pass,* which he followed with the renowned horror story, *Dracula,* in 1897. He went on to write *The Jewel of Seven Stars* (1903) and *The Lair of the White Worm* (1911). With the exception of *Dracula,* Stoker's works were never critically acclaimed.

In his later years, he worked on the literary staff of the London *Telegraph.* He died in 1912.

About the Times

Bram Stoker wrote *Dracula* in 1897. Although no specific year is mentioned in the text, the time can be readily assessed as the latter part of the nineteenth century. This period, commonly referred to as the Victorian period, is so named after Queen Victoria, who reigned supreme in England from 1837-1901. During this time, the British Empire reached its height. Industry flourished, and Britain became known as the workshop of the world. Despite this tremendous growth, there was great suffering among the lower classes.

During the Victorian period, the novel became the most popular literary form among English middle-class readers. Some of the greatest Victorian novelists are Charles Dickens, William Makepeace Thackeray, Thomas Hardy, Emily and Charlotte Brontë, and George Eliot.

In writing *Dracula,* Bram Stoker chose to follow a quintessential British literary tradition. His classic tale of horror contains many elements of the Gothic, a literary genre that is said to have originated in England in 1764 with Horace Walpole's *The Castle of Otranto.* Like most Gothic novels, *Dracula* includes a young woman in distress, a dark villain, and a series of macabre events in a variety of ominous settings.

The Gothic was not the only tradition to impact Stoker's work. Several vampire tales preceded *Dracula* in the 1800s. Sheridan LeFanu's *Carmilla* (1872), in particular, greatly influenced the novel. Furthermore, Stoker based the vampire aspects of the novel on Eastern-European folklore and the character of Count Dracula on Prince Vlad Tepes, a Transylvanian and Wallachian ruler in the mid-fifteenth century.

Teacher's Notes (continued)

Synopsis

This version of *Dracula* is told through an omniscient narrator and the journals and letters of Jonathan and Mina Harker, Dr. John Seward, and Lucy Westenra. The story begins with Jonathan, a young lawyer, traveling from London to Transylvania to conduct business with Count Dracula. Jonathan becomes apprehensive by the fearful attitude of the local people when they discover his plans to visit the Castle Dracula. His anxiety increases over a series of strange occurrences during his journey to, and upon his arrival at, the castle.

Jonathan soon realizes that his host is no ordinary man. The Count, a seemingly bloodless individual, lives alone in the castle and appears only during the hours of darkness. His reflection does not show up in Jonathan's mirror and he is able to crawl up and down the castle walls like a lizard. After a harrowing, dream-like experience involving three ghostly women, Jonathan becomes convinced that the castle is a prison and he is a prisoner.

One day while searching for a way to escape, Jonathan discovers the Count in a ruined chapel under the castle, lying atop one of 50 wooden boxes filled with Transylvanian earth. Fresh blood trickles from the corners of the Count's mouth. While Jonathan remains captive in the castle, the 50 boxes of earth—with the Count in one of them—are hauled off in wagons and eventually delivered to the Count's newly purchased estate of Carfax in Purfleet, England.

After doing away with the entire crew of the *Demeter,* the ship that brought him to England, Count Dracula leaves the ship in Whitby in the form of a wolf. He then proceeds to claim Lucy Westenra, a friend to Mina Murray — Jonathan's fiancée—as a victim. Dr. Seward, a former suitor of Lucy's, is summoned to attend her. He in turn calls on Dr. Abraham Van Helsing, his old professor, for help. Mina leaves for Budapest to join Jonathan, who has been found in need of care in a hospital there. Despite several blood transfusions, Lucy dies and becomes a vampire during Mina's absence. Van Helsing performs a ritualistic operation on Lucy to change her from Un-Dead to truly dead and thereby saves her soul.

Mina and her new husband, Jonathan, return from Budapest and join forces with Seward, Van Helsing, Arthur Holmwood—Lucy's fiancée—and Quincey P. Morris—an American and another former suitor of Lucy's. Together these six hunt for the Count. While basing their search operations at Seward's hospital in Purfleet—adjacent to the Count's Carfax estate—Mina falls victim to the Count. They now know that they must destroy the Count before Mina turns into a vampire.

The men move quickly to find 49 of the 50 boxes of earth scattered about London. In a trance brought on by her blood ties with the Count, Mina tells the others that the remaining box is somewhere at sea: The Count is heading back to Transylvania! The party of six give chase overland on the Orient Express, arriving at the Black Sea port of Varna ahead of the Count's ship. Once in Varna, the Count eludes them and the chase continues. Finally, in the shadow of Castle Dracula, the chase ends. After a bloody scuffle with two Romanian drivers, Quincey and Jonathan overtake a wagon carrying the fiftieth box and send the Count to his just reward. Although the brave Quincey P. Morris dies in the fight, Mina is saved from a vampire's fate.

For convenience, each book has been divided into four study units. This chart shows how the units in the Pacemaker version of *Dracula* correspond to the chapters in the original text.

Study Unit	Pacemaker Classic Chapters	Original Text Chapters
1	1–3	1–4
2	4–5	5–10
3	6–8	11–16
4	9–11	17–27

About the Characters

Count Dracula is a vampire who has lived for hundreds of years from the blood of his victims.

Jonathan Harker is a young English lawyer who travels to Castle Dracula to conduct business with the Count.

Mina Murray is Harker's fiancée; later in the novel she is Mina Harker.

Lucy Westenra is Mina's friend and one of Dracula's victims.

Mrs. Westenra is Lucy's sickly mother.

Dr. John Seward is a doctor who runs a hospital for the mentally ill and is one of Lucy's former suitors.

Dr. Abraham Van Helsing is a Dutch doctor and Seward's former university professor.

Arthur Holmwood is Lucy's fiance.

Lord Godalming is Arthur's father.

Quincey P. Morris is an American soldier of fortune and another of Lucy's former suitors.

Peter Hawkins is an English lawyer and Jonathan's boss.

The three women in the Castle Dracula are vampires.

Audio-Visual Suggestions

- On a world map show some of the places that are mentioned in the story: Vienna, Budapest, the Danube River, London, Transylvania, the Carpathian Mountains, Moldavia (now Moldova), China, England, the Black Sea, and Paris. As these names come up, have students find them again on the map.
- Many movies have been made about *Dracula* and vampires. Tod Browning's 1931 classic, *Dracula,* is the original. It stars Bela Lugosi and sets the image that comes most to mind for the Dracula character. Another *Dracula* in 1974 features Jack Palance in the title role. The most recent version is Francis Ford Coppola's *Dracula,* starring Gary Oldman as the vampire count. Check with your local library or video store to find out whether they're available on video cassette.

Notes on Unit 1

Unit 1 is made up of Chapters 1 through 3. In Chapter 1, the reader meets Jonathan Harker, a young English lawyer. Jonathan is traveling from London to Transylvania to transact the sale of an English estate. The buyer is Count Dracula, a Transylvanian nobleman. Jonathan begins to feel ill at ease when the local folk fear his going to the Castle Dracula. At the Borgo Pass, the Count's carriage arrives to carry Jonathan over the last leg of his trip. An unexpected encounter with a band of wolves increases Jonathan's apprehension. At last, he reaches the dark, gloomy castle of Count Dracula.

In Chapter 2 Jonathan finds his host charming but mysterious. The stark white—almost bloodless—color of Dracula's skin strikes him as unusual, as does the fact that there are no servants in the castle. Business matters must wait until night, as the Count never makes himself available during the day. Jonathan rightly concludes that the castle is a prison, and he is a prisoner.

In Chapter 3, an alarmed Jonathan seeks desperately to find a way out of the castle. After a macabre interlude with three ghost-like women, he discovers 50 large boxes filled with earth in a ruined chapel beneath the castle. The Count is lying on top of one, with blood trickling from the corners of his mouth. Later, the boxes are carted off—with the Count in one of them—and shipped to England. Jonathan is left alone in the castle with no way out.

Unit 1 Project Sheets Answer Key:

Exercise 1: 1. b, c, d, e; 2. c; 3. b, c;
4. Answers will vary.

Exercise 2: A—Answers will vary.
B—Answers will vary.

Exercise 3: A—1. a belief based on fear or ignorance; 2. starvation, a general shortage of food; 3. a residence and the property that surrounds it; 4. a man with a high station or rank in society; 5. any person from whom one is descended; 6. a diary; 7. the woman to whom a man is engaged to be married.
B—Answers will vary.

Exercise 4: A—1. Jonathan; 2. Dracula; 3. old woman at the hotel; 4. Dracula; 5. Jonathan; 6. coach driver; 7. Jonathan.
B—Answers will vary.

Exercise 5: A—1. The coach was moving very fast; 2. The coach lights were moving away; 3. He brought Jonathan and his bags to the front door and left them there; 4. The wolves come out at night; 5. The Count answered directly.
B—Answers will vary.

Exercise 6: A—Answers will vary, but should approximate the following: 1. to ward off evil; 2. he had to do his job; 3. no servants were in the castle; 4. they were afraid to leave their houses; 5. blood tempted the Count; 6. he could only rise at night.
B—Answers to the first parts follow. Answers to the second parts will vary. 3, 5, 6.

Exercise 7: Answers will vary.

Notes on Unit 2

Unit 2 is made up of Chapters 4 and 5. In Chapter 4, Mina Murray, Jonathan Harker's fiancée, visits Lucy Westenra, a childhood friend. Lucy is in Whitby, a seaside town on the Yorkshire coast. Not long after Mina's arrival, a storm strikes the coast, and the *Demeter*—the ship carrying the Count and 50 large boxes to England—is forced into Whitby Harbor. Rescuers find only the dead captain on board, and he is lashed to the wheel. Onlookers sight an enormous dog leaving the beached ship. The ship's log reveals that some sort of *thing* has done away with the entire crew. Later, under mysterious circumstances, both a dog and an old man are found dead.

In Chapter 5, Mina notes that Lucy has taken up her old habit of sleepwalking. One night, Mina finds her on East Cliff, overlooking the harbor. From a distance, Mina sees a long, black figure with a white face and red, gleaming eyes bending over Lucy. The figure disappears before Mina reaches her friend. Mina pins her shawl on Lucy, who is clad only in a nightdress. Later, Mina finds two tiny marks on Lucy's neck and mistakenly thinks she pricked Lucy while pinning on the shawl. When Lucy's health begins to fail, Dr. Seward, a former suitor, is called to attend her. Soon after, Mina leaves for Budapest, where Jonathan has been found in a hospital and in need of help. Seward then calls on his old professor, Dr. Abraham Van Helsing, for help with Lucy. When Lucy fails to respond after two blood transfusions, Van Helsing—an expert in occult matters—prescribes a wreath of garlic.

Unit 2 Project Sheets Answer Key:

Exercise 1: A—Answers to the first parts follow. Answers to the second parts will vary. 1. will; 2. will; 3. will not; 4. will not.
B—Answers will vary.

Exercise 2: A—1. Quincey; 2. Mina; 3. Dracula; 4. Lucy; 5. Van Helsing; 6. Arthur; 7. Billington; 8. Seward.
B—Answers will vary.

Exercise 3: A—1. wedding: a marriage ceremony; 2. another: one more; 3. feeling: an awareness; 4. fishing: catching fish for sport or for a living; 5. funny: amusing; 6. bigger: larger than another; 7. dogging: hunting or tracking; 8. careless: neglectful.
B—Answers will vary.

Exercise 4: A—1. Mina; 2. outside narrator; 3. reporter for *The Dailygraph;* 4. captain of *Demeter* (log); 5. Lucy.
B—Answers will vary.

Exercise 5: A—1. school/teacher, Mina; 2. grave/yard, Dracula; 3. sun/down, Dracula; 4. sleep/walking, Lucy; 5. night/dress, Lucy; 6. moon/light, full moon; 7. every/day, answers will vary.
B—Answers will vary.

Exercise 6: A—(from top) 8; 3; 5; 2; 4; 1; 9; 7; 6.
B—1. 8 & 9; 2. 1 & 2; 3. 3 & 4; 4. 6 & 7; 5. 5 & 6.
C—Answers will vary.

Exercise 7: A—Answers will vary.
B—Answers will vary.

Notes on Unit 3

Unit 3 is made up of Chapters 6 through 8. In Chapter 6, Lucy grows steadily worse. Arthur Holmwood, her fiance, moves her to the Westenra house in Hillingham where Lucy keeps hearing flapping noises outside her window at night. One night, Lucy's mother joins Lucy in her room. Something crashes into the window. The head of a great gray wolf appears in the shattered window. Mrs. Westenra dies of fright on the spot. Not long after, despite another blood transfusion, Lucy dies, too. Seward thinks that at last it is the end for poor Lucy. Van Helsing comments that it is only the beginning.

In Chapter 7, Van Helsing confides that he believes that Lucy has turned into a vampire. He wants to perform a certain ugly procedure on her corpse to free her from the Un-Dead and thereby save her soul. Soon after Lucy's death, several children are found wandering in Hampstead Heath with tiny holes in their throats. Seward thinks that the holes might have been made by whatever made the holes in Lucy's throat. Van Helsing disagrees and tells him that they were put there by Miss Lucy.

In Chapter 8, Van Helsing seeks permission from Arthur Holmwood to "operate" on Lucy's corpse. Arthur consents, and he and Van Helsing, Seward, and Quincey P. Morris—another of Lucy's former suitors—set about the task. When they open Lucy's coffin, they find her in vampire form. Arthur drives a wooden stake through her heart, and Van Helsing and Seward cut off her head. Lucy is Un-Dead no more.

Unit 3 Project Sheets Answer Key:

Exercise 1: A—Suggested answers to the first parts follow. Answers to the second parts will vary. 1. She will die from blood loss; 2. Miss Lucy bit the children; 3. A vampire is killed and becomes *really* dead.
B—Answers will vary.

Exercise 2: A—1. Lucy; 2. Van Helsing; 3. Mina; 4. Seward; 5. Arthur.
B—Answers will vary.

Exercise 3: A—1. coffin: the case or box in which a dead body is buried; 2. trusts: to have confidence in; 3. autopsy: an examination of a dead body; 4. strike: to hit firmly and suddenly; 5. faith: trust; 6. shock: a disorder resulting from poor blood circulation; 7. partner: one who shares a business with others; 8. stake: a piece of wood or metal pointed at one end.
B—Answers will vary.

Exercise 4: 1. very angry (p. 51); 2. time to die herself (p. 52); 3. happy (p. 62); 4. the man to stop Count Dracula (p. 63); 5. shock, trust, permission (p. 68); 6. must kill him (p. 71).

Exercise 5: A—1. angry; 2. sick; 3. afraid.
B—Answers will vary.

Exercise 6: A—Answers to the first parts follow. Answers to the second parts will vary. 1. b; 2. c; 3. d.
B—Answers will vary.

Exercise 7: A—Answers will vary.
B—Answers will vary.

Notes on Unit 4

Unit 4 is made up of Chapters 9 through 11. In Chapter 9, the newly wed Mina and Jonathan Harker join Dr. Seward, Professor Van Helsing, Arthur, and Quincey at Seward's hospital in Purfleet. They vow that together they will seek and destroy Count Dracula. Van Helsing explains the powers and weaknesses of vampires to the others. The men begin looking for the Count's 50 boxes, starting at Carfax, his estate next door to the hospital. While the men search for the boxes, the Count attacks Mina in her room at the hospital. Later, Van Helsing tries to make her pure by touching her forehead with a Holy Wafer. Mina is dismayed when the Wafer burns her skin and leaves a "mark of shame" on her forehead.

In Chapter 10, they know that Mina will become a vampire upon her death unless they destroy the Count. The men continue looking for the boxes, finding all but one. They almost catch the Count in the process, but he escapes. In a trance, Mina reveals to the others that the last box is at sea. The Count is fleeing to Transylvania.

In Chapter 11, the party of six rushes overland to beat the Count's ship to the Black Sea port of Varna. But the Count diverts the ship's course to the inland port of Galatz, temporarily escaping them. Finally, in the shadow of Castle Dracula, they overtake a wagon carrying the fiftieth box. Jonathan and Quincey quickly overcome the drivers and dispatch the Count. At the expense of Quincey's life, Mina's soul is saved. The vampire's curse has passed away.

Unit 4 Project Sheets Answer Key:

Exercise 1: A—Answers will vary.
B—Answers will vary.

Exercise 2: A—Answers will vary.
B—Answers will vary.

Exercise 3: A—1. short/ant; 2. ready/syn; 3. coming/ant; 4. last/ant; 5. fast/ant; 6. brave/ant; 7. stay/syn; 8. sunrise/ant.
B—Answers will vary.

Exercise 4: A—Answers will vary.
B—Answers will vary.

Exercise 5: A—1. They spent some time getting to know each other; 2. I tried to hit it, but I missed; 3. I went to help Mrs. Harker; 4. We found all 12 boxes and fixed them good; 5. But be quick, for the time is short.
B—Answers will vary.

Exercise 6: A—2. Jonathan meets and learns more about Count Dracula; 3. Jonathan realizes that he is a prisoner in the castle; 4. The ship the Count is on arrives in England; 5. Lucy is given a wreath of garlic to ward off the Count; 6. Although she seems dead, Lucy has become a vampire; 7. Lucy takes a few children as her victims; 8. Van Helsing and Arthur "operate" on Lucy's body and save her soul; 9. The Count takes Mina as his next victim; 10. The party of six plan to capture and kill the Count; 11. Quincey dies as he bravely kills the Count and saves Mina from the fate of a vampire.
B—Answers will vary.

Exercise 7: Answers will vary.

Final Exam Answer Key:

A—1. in Europe; 2. to complete the sale of a house; 3. a nobleman; 4. on the *Demeter;* 5. Dr. Seward; 6. garlic flowers; 7. Mina; 8. Carfax. 9. *Czarina Catherine;* 10. Dr. Van Helsing.
B—Answers will vary.

Glossary

advice a suggestion about how to do something

Example: My advice to you is to work harder.

author writer

Example: The author of the book is Bram Stoker.

author's purpose the special reason an author has for writing a story or book

Example: The author's purpose in writing the book was to tell about vampires.

brainstorm to list ideas as fast as they come, without commenting on or organizing them in any way; usually done by a group of people working together

Example: The children brainstormed until they had a list of 50 ideas.

cause anything which produces an effect, action, or result

Example: A virus was the cause of his illness.

character a person in a story

Example: Dr. Seward is an important character in *Dracula.*

chart a graph or some other visual way of presenting information

Example: This chart lists the symptoms and treatments of five childhood diseases.

comparison a way of showing how two things are alike or different

Example: The comparison showed that this red is much brighter than that one.

conflict a battle or struggle; the opposition of two forces or ideas

Example: The conflict between the father and his son involved using the car without permission.

context clues hints in a sentence or paragraph that help tell what an unknown word means

Example: Through context clues, Wesley figured out that *enormous* means the same as *huge.*

conversation talking; an oral exchange of ideas between two or more people

Example: Darlene and Darryl had a long conversation about the book.

coöperative learning group a small group of students who work together to share knowledge and help one another learn

Example: Alice learned better study habits from her cooperative learning group.

diagram a type of chart; a way of showing something visually so it's easier to understand

Example: This diagram will show you how to put the chair together.

dialogue the words that characters in a story say to each other

Example: The author has written some very funny dialogue in the second chapter.

diary a written record of a person's experiences or thoughts

Example: Janette wrote in her diary every day.

effect a direct result

Example: The effect of lying in the sun for too long can be a bad sunburn.

epilogue a short section at the end of a story; it often takes place well after the main events

Example: The epilogue described the lives of the characters ten years after they got married.

Glossary (continued)

frame story a story within a story

Example: A frame story often has a long introduction.

introduction the opening part of a story

Example: The introduction to the story explained how the writer thought of the idea for it.

journal a daily record of activities or thoughts; similar to a diary

Example: Tom kept a journal on his trip to Europe.

motive a reason for doing something

Example: His motive for working at two jobs was to earn extra money to buy a new car.

opinion something that a person believes is true

Example: Mick's opinion was that the area was dangerous.

passage a line or several lines from a story or book

Example: That passage from the novel was difficult to understand.

plot the events that take place in a story

Example: The plot was very simple: man trains for race, man runs race, man wins race.

point of view the position or angle from which someone sees something

Example: The point of view was through the eyes of an outside observer.

prediction what someone says is going to happen

Example: Jo's prediction was that it would rain.

prologue part of the story that comes before the main action; an introduction

Example: In the prologue the author introduces the reader to the main character.

quotation the exact words that someone says

Example: Here is a quotation from the speech: "No new taxes!"

sequence the order in which something happens

Example: The sequence of events led to the capture of the criminal.

setting the place and time of a story or event

Example: The setting of the story was San Francisco during the Gold Rush days.

simile a comparison using the words *like* or *as*

Example: He ran like a rabbit.

symbol something that stands for something else

Example: The flag is a symbol of our country.

Setting the Scene

Exercise **1**

The **setting** of a story is the place and time in which the action happens. The setting of *Dracula* is various countries in Europe sometime in the late 1800s. At the time of this story, automobiles, electric lights, telephones, televisions, computers, and airplanes had not yet been invented. People traveled on foot, on horseback, by horse-drawn carriage, by train, and by ship. They kept in touch with others and the world by means of letters, telegrams, and newspapers.

Use the information about the setting to answer the following questions. For questions 1–3, put a check next to the best answer or answers. For question 4, write your answer on the lines.

1. Jonathan Harker traveled most of the way from London to Transylvania by train. How else might he have traveled?

   a. ______ by airplane b. ______ by carriage

   c. ______ by horse d. ______ by ship

   e. ______ on foot f. ______ by bus

2. Jonathan sent letters from Eastern Europe to Mr. Hawkins and Mina Murray in England. How else might he have kept in touch with them?

   a. ______ by telephone b. ______ by fax

   c. ______ by telegram d. ______ by computer mail

3. The people living in Europe at the time of this story stayed in touch with the rest of the world by:

   a. ______ listening to the radio b. ______ reading magazines

   c. ______ reading newspapers d. ______ watching television

4. Imagine that you are in a small village in the mountains of Transylvania during the late 1800s. You want to visit your friends in London, England. How will you get there? Describe at least two ways.

   ____

   ____

   ____

Prereading

Exercise 2

A. In the book you are about to read, the main character is Count Dracula. He is a vampire. Legend has it that a vampire is an "Un-Dead" creature that feeds off the blood of others. Dracula himself is several hundred years old. He has lived that long by sucking the blood from many victims. When his victims die, they become vampires, too. What do you think would happen in the world if vampires really existed? Write your answer on the lines below.

____

____

____

____

____

____

B. Think of someone that you know and like. Now imagine that this person became a vampire. How do you think this person would change? What would this person look like? What would this person act like? Would you still feel the same way about this person? Why or why not? Write your answer on the lines below. Use the back of this sheet if you need more room.

____

____

____

____

____

____

____

____

Key Words

Exercise 3

A. Read the sentences below. Use context clues to make a good guess at what the words in dark type mean. Write the meanings on the lines.

1. Jonathan Harker learned of many **superstitions** while traveling to Transylvania. One old woman told him that evil takes power over the world on St. George's Eve.

   A **superstition** is ______________________________

2. In the 17th century, the city of Bistritz lost many people to war, **famine,** and disease. Jonathan could see signs of the death, hunger, and illness that had once plagued the city.

   Famine means ______________________________

3. Jonathan's business was about the sale of an **estate** in England. The estate was called Carfax. The Count was going to move there.

   An **estate** is ______________________________

4. Count Dracula was a **nobleman.** "Dracula" was his family name. "Count" was his title.

   A **nobleman** is ______________________________

5. Whenever the Count spoke about his **ancestors,** he always said "we." He talked about his relatives from the past as if he were alive at the same time they were.

   An **ancestor** is ______________________________

6. Jonathan kept a **journal** in which he wrote about many of the things that happened to him. He wrote in his journal almost every day.

   Another name for a **journal** is ______________________________

7. Mina Murray, Jonathan's **fiancée,** would want to hear all about his trip to Transylvania. After all, she planned to marry Jonathan very soon.

   A **fiancée** is ______________________________

B. Use a dictionary to look up the meaning of each word in dark type. How close were your guesses? Now choose three of the words in dark type from Part A. On the back of this sheet, write a paragraph in which you use each word at least once.

Point of View

A. This story is told from several points of view. Some parts are told through journal entries, letters, and telegrams of certain characters. Other parts are told by an outside narrator. Because people are different, they look at things in different ways. Read the sentences below. These sentences are not from the story, but they could be. On the lines provided, write which character might have said them.

1. The food in Klausenburgh tasted very good but it made me thirsty.

______

2. My family history goes back to Attila the Hun.

______

3. Many bad things can happen on St. George's eve.

______

4. I love to listen to the music that the wolves make.

______

5. Sometimes I wish that Mr. Hawkins made the trip instead of me.

______

6. I whipped the horses because the Englishman was in a hurry.

______

7. There doesn't seem to be any way out of here.

______

B. Why do you think the author used journal entries, letters, and telegrams to tell this story? Would the story have been better if told by only the outside narrator? Why or why not? Write your answers below.

______

______

______

______

Language Lab

A. Authors sometimes use words and phrases that do not mean exactly what they say. The numbered sentences are from the story. Read each one. Then put a check mark next to the sentence below it that best explains the word or phrase in dark type. The page numbers tell where you can find the sentences in the book.

1. No matter how bad the road, the coach seemed to **fly over** it in a great hurry. (page 5)
   ______ The coach had wings.
   ______ The coach didn't touch the ground.
   ______ The coach was moving very fast.
2. Jonathan looked back and saw the **lights of the other coach growing smaller**. (page 7)
   ______ The coach lights were shrinking.
   ______ The coach lights were moving away.
   ______ The battery for the coach lights was running down.
3. Dracula's driver **dropped off** Jonathan and his bags at the front door to the castle. (page 10)
   ______ He let Jonathan and his bags fall from the top of the coach.
   ______ He was standing on Jonathan and his bags when the driver jumped down from the coach.
   ______ He brought Jonathan and his bags to the front door and left them there.
4. Listen to them—**the children of the night.** (page 12)
   ______ The wolves come out at night.
   ______ The wolves are young.
   ______ The night is mother and father to the wolves.
5. Sometimes the Count answered **straight out.** Other times not. (page 14)
   ______ The Count's body lay out straight when he answered.
   ______ The Count answered directly.
   ______ The Count went outside to answer.

B. In the future, people might not understand some of the words and phrases that we use today. Write a few words and phrases that you use that do not mean exactly what they say. Then explain what they really mean. Use the back of this sheet to do your work.

Character Study

Exercise
6

A. Very often you can learn a lot about a character by what he or she does in the story. Why do you think the characters in this story did the following things? Give reasons based on what you have read so far.

1. An old woman gave Jonathan the cross from around her neck for him to wear. ______________________________

____

2. Jonathan went to the Castle Dracula even though he was beginning to feel afraid. ______________________________

____

3. The Count fixed supper and made the bed for Jonathan. ______________

____

4. The people in Transylvania didn't come out to look for buried gold on St. George's Eve. ______________________________

____

5. The Count told Jonathan to be careful about cutting himself. __________

____

____

6. The Count was always away during the day. ______________________

____

B. Which of the following statements about Count Dracula do you think are true? Put a check mark next to each one. Then on the back of this sheet, write two true statements of your own about the Count.

______ 1. Count Dracula is a harmless man.
______ 2. Count Dracula enjoys having supper with Jonathan.
______ 3. Count Dracula knows a lot about Transylvanian history.
______ 4. Count Dracula likes to spend the afternoons with Jonathan.
______ 5. Count Dracula keeps most of the doors in the castle locked.
______ 6. Count Dracula is a man with many secrets.

Challenge

Knowing the following facts can help you better understand the story of *Dracula.* Think about these facts as you answer the questions below.

- The story of *Dracula* was based on a legend. And the legend was based on real life happenings. This doesn't mean that vampires really exist. It does mean that there is some truth in almost all fiction.
- The character of Count Dracula was based on a real person who lived in the fifteenth century. His name was Prince Vlad Tepes.
- The prince ruled over Transylvania and Wallachia (now Romania). During his rule, he killed many people by stabbing them with wooden sticks.
- His people called him "The Impaler." They thought he liked the sight of blood so much that he must be a vampire. The prince took the name of *Dracula* from the legend and made it his own.

1. In what ways is Count Dracula like Prince Vlad Tepes?

____

____

____

____

2. In what ways is he different from Prince Vlad Tepes?

____

____

____

____

3. Does knowing that the character of Dracula is based on a real person make him more frightening? Why or why not?

____

____

____

____

Prereading

Exercise

1

A. Chapters 1–3 introduced three of the main characters: Jonathan Harker, Mina Murray, and Count Dracula. The following sentences tell what might happen to these characters in the rest of the novel. Write *will* or *will not* on the lines below. Then give reasons for your answers.

1. The Count ____________ travel by ship to England.

   The reason I think so is because ______________________________

   ____

2. Jonathan ____________ escape from the castle.

   The reason I think so is because ______________________________

   ____

3. Jonathan ____________ become a vampire.

   The reason I think so is because ______________________________

   ____

4. The Count ____________ change his ways and become a nice man.

   The reason I think so is because ______________________________

   ____

B. Look ahead to the title of Chapter 4. Think about what might happen next. Write your ideas below.

____

____

____

____

____

____

Character Study

A. Each sentence below describes a character in the story. Read each one. On the line, write the name of the person who is being described. Choose from the following names: Van Helsing, Lucy, Seward, Arthur, Dracula, Mina, Quincey, Billington.

1. He is an American from Texas. ______________________

2. She is a schoolteacher. ______________________

3. He owns an estate called Carfax. ______________________

4. She will be 20 in September. ______________________

5. He is a doctor and a professor. ______________________

6. He is the son of an English lord. ______________________

7. He is a Whitby lawyer. ______________________

8. He runs a hospital for the mentally ill. ______________________

B. On the lines provided, write two words of your own that describe each character listed below.

Van Helsing ______________ ______________

Lucy ______________ ______________

Seward ______________ ______________

Mina ______________ ______________

Key Words

Exercise 3

Some words are made of root words with word parts added. The word parts can be **prefixes** or **suffixes.** They change the meaning of the root word.

A. Look at the root words below. The page numbers tell where in the book you can find that root word with a prefix or suffix added to it. Write the whole word. Then write its meaning. Use context clues from the sentences in the story, or look the word up in a dictionary.

1. wed (page 31) ______________________________

____

2. other (page 32) ______________________________

____

3. feel (page 33) ______________________________

____

4. fish (page 34) ______________________________

____

5. fun (page 34) ______________________________

____

6. big (page 34) ______________________________

____

7. dog (page 37) ______________________________

____

8. care (page 41) ______________________________

B. Find four more words in the book that are made up of a root word and a prefix or suffix. Write them below.

______________________________ ______________________________

______________________________ ______________________________

Exercise 4

Point of View

A. Chapters 4 and 5 are told through five different points of view. Look over these chapters again. Then list the different points of view on the lines below.

1. ______________________________
2. ______________________________
3. ______________________________
4. ______________________________
5. ______________________________

B. Imagine that you lived in Whitby when the sailing ship *Demeter* was forced into the harbor there. Think about the storm and the heavy seas. Think about the dead captain that was found on the ship and the large dog that fled the ship. Then write a paragraph about what you saw on the lines below.

____

____

____

____

____

____

____

____

____

____

____

____

____

Language Lab

A. The words in dark type are **compound words.** They are made up of two shorter words. Write the two words that make up each compound word below. Then answer the questions that follow.

1. **schoolteacher** ______________________
   Who in this story is a schoolteacher?
   ____

2. **graveyard** ______________________
   Who in this story is most likely to be found in a graveyard?
   ____

3. **sundown** ______________________
   Who in this story would you not expect to see before sundown?
   ____

4. **sleepwalking** ______________________
   Who in this story has a habit of sleepwalking?
   ____

5. **nightdress** ______________________
   Who in this story wears a nightdress much of the time?
   ____

6. **moonlight** ______________________
   What do we call the moon when it looks like a complete circle?
   ____

7. **everyday** ______________________
   Name something that you do everyday.
   ____

B. We all use compound words everyday. On the back of this sheet, list five common compound words. Write a sentence for each word.

Exercise
6

Plot and Sequence

A. The following events all happened in Chapters 4 and 5 of the story. But they are out of order. Write numbers from 1 to 9 on the lines to show the correct sequence of events.

_________ Dr. Seward asked Professor Van Helsing for help with Lucy.

_________ A large dog jumped off the *Demeter* and ran out of sight.

_________ Mina found Lucy sleepwalking on East Cliff.

_________ Lucy told Mina about three men who proposed to her.

_________ A reporter learned that the *Demeter* was a Russian ship.

_________ Mina arrived in Whitby.

_________ Professor Van Helsing gave Lucy a wreath of garlic.

_________ Dr. Seward was called in to look at Lucy.

_________ Lucy's mother learned that she didn't have long to live.

B. Where do the following events fit in the sequence above?

1. Dr. Seward gave blood to Lucy.

   This happened between _____ and _____
2. Lucy and Mina went from the train station to The Crescent.

   This happened between _____ and _____
3. The captain of the *Demeter* was found dead on his ship.

   This happened between _____ and _____
4. Mina left Whitby to go to Jonathan in Budapest.

   This happened between _____ and _____
5. Mina and Lucy saw a large bat flying in rings around the yard.

   This happened between _____ and _____

C. Professor Van Helsing didn't tell anyone why he ordered garlic flowers for Lucy. Do you think he should have told Dr. Seward his reasons right then? Why or why not? Write your answer on the back of this sheet.

Challenge

A. Reread the notes from the log of the *Demeter* on pages 37 and 38. The captain had a duty to remain with his ship. The last entry in the log didn't tell what happened to the captain. But when the ship came ashore, the captain was found dead. What do *you* think happened? Write a paragraph telling how you think the captain died.

B. Imagine that you were the captain of the *Demeter.* What would you have done that the captain didn't do? What would you *not* have done that the captain *did* do. Write your answers below.

Exercise 1

Prereading

A. Listed below are the titles of Chapters 6, 7, and 8. Think about what might happen next in the story. Read the following choices. Put a check mark by the one that seems most likely. Then give a reason for your choice.

1. Chapter 6: Only the Beginning
   What do you think will happen to Lucy Westenra?
   ______ She will die from blood loss.
   ______ She will scare off the vampire with a kitchen knife.
   ______ She will get killed falling off East Cliff.
   ______ She will kill the vampire with a silver bullet.
   Why do you think this is the most likely choice? ______________________

   ____

2. Chapter 7: The Hampstead Horror
   Several missing children are found in Hampstead Heath. They all have tiny holes in their throats. What do you think caused them?
   ______ They scratched themselves playing in the bushes.
   ______ Count Dracula bit the children.
   ______ They were bitten by rats that live in the heath.
   ______ Miss Lucy bit the children.
   Why do you think this is the most likely choice? ______________________

   ____

3. Chapter 8: Un-Dead No More
   Vampires exist somewhere between life and death in a state called the "un-dead." The title of this chapter suggests one of the following things:
   ______ A main character dies and comes back to life.
   ______ A vampire is killed and becomes *really* dead.
   ______ There are no vampires left in the world.
   ______ A vampire starts life all over again.
   Why do you think this is the most likely choice? ______________________

   ____

B. Vampires exist between two states of being. They are not alive, nor are they truly dead. Can you think of a time in your own life when you felt "caught in the middle" of two things? How did you feel about it? Write your answer on the back of this sheet. If you prefer, write about an imaginary situation.

Character Study

A. The following lines of dialogue do not appear in the book. But suppose they did. Which character do you think would have said each one? Write the name of the character on the line.

1. "I love most animals. But that bird flapping around outside my window all night is beginning to keep me awake. And that dog howling in the bushes doesn't help any."

   ____

2. "I have known you since you were a student in my class. I never told you anything then that was not true. I would not tell you anything now that is not true. You must trust me."

   ____

3. "I am so glad that the professor has agreed to read our journals. Maybe he can make some sense out of all this. So many strange things have happened, I don't know *what* to believe anymore."

   ____

4. "At first I thought he had gone mad. I know how thin the line is that separates us all from madness. On second thought, he always has a good reason for everything he does."

   ____

5. "It was probably the hardest thing I ever had to do. How do you ask a person to do something like that to someone so dear. But there was no other way to save her soul."

   ____

B. Choose one of the sets of sentences above and add to it. You may want to write an imaginary conversation between two characters. Or you may want to write one character's thoughts in the form of a diary entry. Try to give a good description of what the characters are thinking and feeling. Use the back of this sheet to do your work.

Key Words

Exercise
3

A. The following words are found in Chapters 6 through 8. Read each sentence below and use context clues to figure out which word belongs with that sentence. Write the word in the blank. Then write its meaning on the line below. You may use a dictionary if necessary.

partner (page 57)	faith (page 60)	coffin (page 66)	stake (page 69)
autopsy (page 59)	shock (page 64)	trusts (page 68)	strike (page 70)

1. Again he took the cover off Lucy's ____________.

____

2. My good friend Jack Seward ____________ you with his life.

____

3. Must we do an ____________ on that poor woman's body?

____

4. ____________ to drive away the Un-Dead.

____

5. You must have ____________ in me.

____

6. [She died] from the ____________ of losing all that blood.

____

7. Jonathan is now a full ____________ in the law firm of Hawkins & Harker.

____

8. Put the ____________ to her heart.

____

B. Look through Chapters 6 through 8 again. Pick out four words that you think some students might not know. Write a definition for each one, using your own words. Then use the word in a sentence that would help these students better understand it. Write your definitions and sentences on the back of this sheet.

Point of View

Exercise 4

Explain each character's point of view about the following subjects. Write your answers on the lines. Then tell where you found this information in the book.

1. What is Van Helsing's point of view about Mrs. Westenra removing the garlic flowers from Lucy's room? ______________________________

   ____

   I found this on page or pages ______________________________

2. What is Lucy's point of view about herself after her mother dies?

   ____

   ____

   I found this on page or pages ______________________________

3. What is Mina's point of view about meeting Dr. Van Helsing?

   ____

   ____

   I found this on page or pages ______________________________

4. What is Jonathan's point of view about Dr. Van Helsing?

   ____

   ____

   I found this on page or pages ______________________________

5. What is Arthur's point of view about what Van Helsing wanted to do to Lucy's body? ______________________________

   ____

   I found this on page or pages ______________________________

6. What is Dr. Van Helsing's point of view concerning Count Dracula?

   ____

   ____

   I found this on page or pages ______________________________

Language Lab

Exercise 5

A. Writers sometimes use description to tell how a character feels. Read this example:
After another hour, Lucy woke from her sleep, fresh and bright. (page 51)

Read the sentences below. Then put a check mark next to the best answer.

1. Dr. Seward watched Van Helsing's face turn a deep red. The professor was trying very hard to keep a hold on his feelings. He could not reveal his thoughts to a woman with a bad heart. (page 51)

   This shows that Professor Van Helsing is feeling

   ______ angry ______ sick
   ______ embarrassed ______ hot
   ______ afraid ______ thrilled

2. Lucy's face looked still more white and drawn. The two holes in her throat were bigger and ringed with a white coating. (page 54)

   This means that Lucy is feeling

   ______ frightened ______ shocked
   ______ sick ______ tired
   ______ sad ______ upset

3. All at once, Jonathan cried out, "My God!" He was looking at a tall, thin man with a hooked nose and a pointed mustache. (page 60)

   This means that Jonathan is feeling

   ______ disappointed ______ afraid
   ______ disgusted ______ relieved
   ______ hopeful ______ happy

B. Think about a person who is feeling a strong emotion. It might be happiness, sadness, fear, disappointment, or anything else you choose. Write a brief paragraph *showing* the emotion without *telling* the reader what the emotion is. Give only enough clues to help the reader figure it out. Write your answer on the back of this sheet.

Supporting Details

A. Read each group of sentences below. The sentence in dark type is the *main idea* of the story. The other sentences should be *details* that back up the main idea. There is one sentence in each group that does *not* back up the main idea. Cross out that sentence. Then write another sentence that *does* back up the main idea.

1. **Count Dracula was a vampire who lived on the blood of others.**
   a. The Count was several hundred years old.
   b. The Count would not hurt animals.
   c. The Count claimed Jonathan as a victim for a short time.
   d. The Count drained Lucy's blood several times.

   ___

   ___

2. **Count Dracula was feared by all who knew him.**
   a. Lucy's mother dropped dead when she saw him as a wolf.
   b. Van Helsing was afraid of the Count but ready to fight him.
   c. Jonathan thought the Count was a nice man at heart.
   d. The Count did away with the crew of the *Demeter.*

   ___

   ___

3. **The Count could change himself into different forms.**
   a. He sometimes took the form of a wolf.
   b. He often turned himself into a bat.
   c. Once in a while he changed himself into a fog or mist.
   d. He could only change forms in Transylvania.

   ___

   ___

B. Choose one of the sentences below as the main idea of a paragraph. Then add details to back up the main idea. Write your paragraph on the back of this sheet.

1. The Count chose Lucy as his first victim in England.
2. Professor Van Helsing was the first to understand what was wrong with Lucy.

Challenge

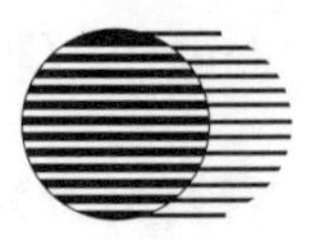

A. Professor Van Helsing is one of the strongest characters in the story of *Dracula.* He is also probably the wisest. Because he understood about vampires, he was almost able to save Lucy. When she died, he knew what needed to be done to save her soul. What might have happened if Dr. Seward had not called on the professor for help? Write a paragraph below describing how the story might have been different.

B. Most people don't know anything about vampires. They might think that Professor Van Helsing's methods for saving Lucy's soul were extreme. Imagine that you are Arthur Holmwood. What would you tell the professor after he describes what he wants to do with Lucy? Write your answer below and explain it.

Prereading

Exercise 1

A. How does an author keep a reader interested in a story? One way is to leave important questions unanswered. The reader keeps reading to find out the answers to the questions. You are about to read the final three chapters of *Dracula.* First read the questions below. Then write what you think the answers will be. Explain the reasons for your answers.

1. Where is Count Dracula now? What happened to him?

____

____

2. Why did Count Dracula come to England?

____

____

3. Why did he bring 50 boxes of Transylvanian earth with him? What happened to them?

____

____

4. What role does Mina Harker play in the rest of the story?

____

____

5. What happens to Count Dracula?

____

____

B. Save this sheet of paper. After you finish reading the story, look over your answers. Did you predict correctly?

Character Study

Exercise 2

A. The list of words can be used to describe different characters from the story. Think about each character named below. Then write a sentence describing that character. Use at least one of the words in the list in each sentence. You may want to use some words more than once.

beautiful	strong	wicked	brave
wise	handsome	loving	ugly
noble	weak	loyal	sneaky
innocent	foolish	honest	sickly

1. Count Dracula ______________________________

____

____

2. Mina Harker ______________________________

____

____

3. Quincey P. Morris ______________________________

____

____

4. Dr. John Seward ______________________________

____

____

5. Jonathan Harker ______________________________

____

____

B. Use one of your sentences as the basis for a detailed description of one of the characters. Tell what the character is like. Then support each of your statements with an example from the story. Write your description on the back of this sheet.

Key Words

A. The sentences below are from the book. But one word in each sentence is wrong. Find the sentence in the book. On this sheet, cross out the wrong word and write the correct word above it. On the line, write *antonym* if the wrong word is the *opposite* of the correct word. Write *synonym* if the wrong word has the same meaning as the correct word. You may use a dictionary.

1. He talked for a long while with Dr. Seward. (page 73)

____

2. Now everything would be prepared when Dr. Van Helsing came back. (page 73)

____

3. His power leaves him at the going of the day. (page 74)

____

4. When we find the first box, we will find our vampire. (page 75)

____

5. But the Count moved too slowly. (page 81)

____

6. What a cowardly man is Quincey! (page 85)

____

7. No, he must remain in the box. (page 86)

____

8. Mina and Van Helsing got to the Borgo Pass just after sundown. (page 88)

____

B. Write two words that are synonyms of each other. Then write two words that are antonyms of each other.

______________ ______________

______________ ______________

Point of View

A. Imagine that Count Dracula has been caught. He is on trial for killing Lucy Westenra. Do you think he would plead guilty or not guilty? What would he say in his defense? What would Professor Van Helsing say? What would Arthur Holmwood say? Write your answers on the lines below.

Count Dracula:

I plead ________________ to the charges against me. This is what I have to say in my defense:

____

____

____

____

Professor Van Helsing:

I treated Miss Lucy for her illness and know what caused her death. This is what I have to say about the case:

____

____

____

____

Arthur Holmwood:

Lucy was my fiancée. I know all about how and why she died. This is what I have to say about the case:

____

____

____

____

B. Suppose you were a lawyer at the trial. Would you defend Count Dracula, or would you tell the court to punish him? What would you say to make the judge and jury agree with you? On the back of this sheet, write a paragraph explaining your answer.

Language Lab

Exercise 5

A. The sentences below are not in the book. But there are sentences in the book that mean the same thing. Read each sentence below. Notice the page number. Look on that page in the book and find the sentence that means the same thing. Write it on the line.

1. They spent some time getting acquainted. (page 72)

___

2. I tried to shoot it, but my aim was off. (page 75)

___

3. I went to the aid of Mrs. Harker. (page 79)

___

4. We took care of the 12 boxes. (page 80)

___

5. But be fast about it, because we are running out of time. (page 82)

___

B. You use many expressions to help you describe things or show your feelings. Think of four expressions that you use often. On the lines below, use these four expressions in sentences of your own.

___

___

___

___

___

___

___

___

___

Stating Main Ideas

A. Chapter titles often give hints about the main events in a chapter. Read the chapter titles below from *Dracula.* Use the titles to help you state the main idea of each chapter. The first one has been done for you.

Chapter 1: The Dark Castle

Jonathan Harker arrives at the forbidding castle of Count Dracula.

Chapter 2: The Count

Chapter 3: No Way Out

Chapter 4: Wreck of the *Demeter*

Chapter 5: Wreath of Garlic

Chapter 6: Only the Beginning

Chapter 7: The Hampstead Horror

Chapter 8: Un-Dead No More

Chapter 9: Mark of Shame

Chapter 10: Running Out of Time

Chapter 11: Death of a Brave Man

B. Pick one of the chapters listed above. Use the back of this sheet to write a summary of that chapter. Begin with your main idea. Then add the important details.

Challenge

> Imagine that you could write a letter to Bram Stoker about his book, *Dracula.* What would you tell him? What would you ask? You may complete the form below. Or you may write your own letter on the back of this sheet.

Dear Bram Stoker:

I have just read the story of Dracula. In general, this is what I thought of it:

____

I thought Count Dracula was: ______________________________

I thought Professor Van Helsing was: ______________________________

____

This is what I thought of some of the other characters: ______________

____

My favorite part of the book was: ______________________________

____

I liked that part because: ______________________________

____

The most surprising part of the story for me was: ______________

____

It was surprising because: ______________________________

If I could change anything in the story, this is what I would change:

____

I would like to know your opinion of these things: ______________

____

If you could write another story, I wish you would write about: ________

____

Sincerely,

____

Final Exam, page 1

A. Put a check mark next to the best answer.

1. Where does the story take place?
   - ☐ in Africa
   - ☐ in Asia
   - ☐ in Europe
   - ☐ in America

2. Why did Jonathan go to Transylvania to see the Count?
   - ☐ to arrest him
   - ☐ to complete the sale of a house
   - ☐ to buy Castle Dracula
   - ☐ to sell magazines

3. Count Dracula was
   - ☐ a nobleman
   - ☐ a lawyer
   - ☐ a doctor
   - ☐ a thief

4. How did the Count travel to England?
   - ☐ by automobile
   - ☐ on the *Demeter*
   - ☐ flying in the form of a bat
   - ☐ on the *Orient Express*

5. Who asked Professor Van Helsing to look at Lucy?
   - ☐ Mina
   - ☐ Mrs. Westenra
   - ☐ Arthur
   - ☐ Dr. Seward

6. What did Van Helsing use to keep the vampire away from Lucy?
   - ☐ a sword
   - ☐ a guard dog
   - ☐ a barbed-wire fence
   - ☐ garlic flowers

7. Who was the Count's next victim after Lucy?
   - ☐ Mina
   - ☐ Arthur
   - ☐ Jonathan
   - ☐ Van Helsing

8. What was the name of the Count's estate in England?
   - ☐ Hillingham
   - ☐ Carfax
   - ☐ Purfleet
   - ☐ Bermondsey

9. What was the name of the ship that carried the Count to Galatz?
   - ☐ *Demeter*
   - ☐ *Exeter*
   - ☐ *Czarina Catherine*
   - ☐ *Golden Hind*

10. Which of the following men was not married at the end of the book?
    - ☐ Arthur
    - ☐ Dr. Van Helsing
    - ☐ Dr. Seward
    - ☐ Jonathan

Final Exam, page 2

B. Write two sentences about each of the following characters. In the first one, tell how the person knows about or comes in contact with Count Dracula. In the second one, tell about a quality of that character's personality.

1. Jonathan

____

____

2. Mina

____

____

3. Lucy

____

____

4. Dr. Seward

____

____

5. Dr. Van Helsing

____

____

6. Arthur

____

____

7. Quincey

____

____

Choose Your Own Project

Choose one project from each section.

Alone:

- Reread the description of Count Dracula in the second chapter of the novel. Then draw a picture of him. You may wish to compare your picture to the illustrations in the book or to photographs of actors who have played Dracula in the movies.
- What do you think is the most dramatic moment of the story? Show or describe that moment in some way. You can draw or paint it, write an essay about it, or even write a poem or a song about it.

With a partner:

- Write sentences that might have been said by a character in the book. The sentences should give clues to the character. Have your partner guess who said each one. If your partner has trouble guessing, you might have to make up new clues.
- Play "What if?" Ask your partner what if something had happened differently in the book. For example, what if, after Lucy died, Count Dracula had not chosen Mina as his next victim? Your partner should tell you how the story might have changed. Take turns asking the "what if" questions.

With a group:

- Watch one or more of the movies about *Dracula* together as a group. Notice the ways in which the films follow Bram Stoker's story. Notice the ways in which they are different from the story. Why do you think the movie makers made these changes? Decide as a group which movie version is the best. Then, write a review of that movie to share with the rest of the class.
- Research what life was like in England in the late 1800s. Each person in the group should research a different aspect of life, such as what people wore, what they ate, where they lived, what jobs they had, and how they entertained themselves. Then combine your reports and present your findings to the class.

Working with the Glossary

Before completing this page, you may wish to look once more at the glossary your teacher has given you. Review the definitions of any of the terms used below.

Comparisons Find two comparisons the author makes to give you a dramatic picture of a character, scene, or event.

____

____

____

____

Conflict Find at least one example of a conflict between two characters or between a character and an event. Then find one example of a conflict *within* a character.

____

____

____

____

Dialogue Find at least two lines of dialogue that best express the hopes of two of the major characters in the story.

Character 1: ____

____

____

Character 2: ____

____

____

Point of View From whose point of view was this story told? (Which character?)

____

Choose another major character in the story. Then describe how the story might have been different if it had been told from this character's point of view. Use the back of this sheet.

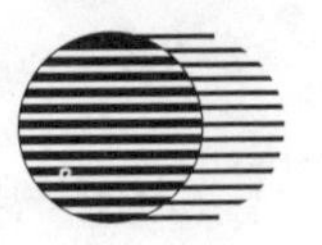

Sequencing the Story

List six events from the book in the sequence in which they occurred. Then cut out the six boxes below and exchange them with a classmate. Now take your classmate's work and arrange those boxes in the correct sequence of events. When you're done, check each other's work.

Understanding the Times, page 1

Time and place shape our lives. People who lived 200 years ago faced different circumstances than we do now. They did different work, listened to different music, and had a different view of the world. And people who live in busy crowded places have always looked at life differently than people who live in far-off country corners.

Story characters also exist in a framework of time and place. Where and when the story unfolds often determine the events the characters must deal with. This exercise will deepen your understanding of how the events of the story were influenced by the time and place. In order to complete the exercise, you may need to do research outside the classroom.

PART A GEOGRAPHY/HISTORY

1. About how many years ago does the story take place? ________________

2. In what century does the story take place? ____________________________

   In what year or years? ________________

3. Was this a time of peace or war? Of plenty or want? Of freedom or lack of freedom? Write three sentences to describe the mood of the time.

   ____

   ____

   ____

4. In what country does the story take place? ____________________________

   In what city or region? ____

   Was this a real city or a fictional one? ______________________________

5. Who was the leader of the country at this time? ______________________

PART B THE ARTS

1. Name three famous artists from the era (time period) in which the story takes place. ______________________________

   ______________________________ ______________________________

2. Name one famous painting by each artist named above.

   ______________________________ ______________________________

   ____

Understanding the Times, page 2

3. What type of music were people listening to at the time of the story?

____

4. Name two famous composers or musicians from the era of the story.

_____________________ _____________________

5. Name one famous musical piece for each person named above.

_____________________ _____________________

PART C DAILY LIFE

Take two of the major characters from the story and answer the questions below.

1. What kinds of work did these characters do?

_____________________ _____________________

2. Do people today do the same kinds of work?

____

3. Choose one of the two characters from above. Write a paragraph explaining how his or her job has changed from what it was back then to what it is today. Write on the back of this sheet or on another sheet of paper.

4. Write a paragraph describing each item below. Write on the back of this sheet or on another sheet of paper.
   (a) a typical day of work for the character chosen above;
   (b) a typical day of work for a person today who has the same job;
   (c) a typical evening at home for the character chosen above;
   (d) a typical evening at home for someone today who has a similar lifestyle as the character above.